THE YETI FILES

Monsters on the Run

KEVIN SHERRY

To my parents—thanks for
all the art lessons.

ISBN 978-0-545-91072-9

10 9 8 7 6 5 4 3 2 1   15 16 17 18 19

Printed in the U.S.A. 23
First printing 2015

Book design by Carol Ly

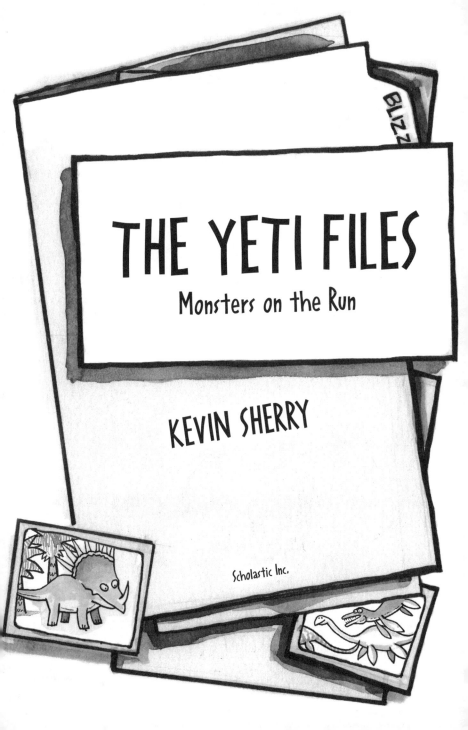

THE YETI FILES

Monsters on the Run

KEVIN SHERRY

Scholastic Inc.

Thanks to Teresa Kietlinski, R. M. O'Brien, Ryan Patterson, Rachel Valsing, Dalen Beran, Jordan Card, Lisa Krause, Ed Schrader, Dan Deacon, Lizz King, and James Petz.

Chapter 1:
A GOOD LESSON

There's nothing better than playing with your pals.

Frank, Noodles...
fetch!

We'll fix it later. Right now, everyone come inside. Cousin Brian and I want to show you an important game.

Strength, money, and luck

can only get you so far in life.

We cryptids have to **use our brains** to protect ourselves.

This game will help you think fast.
It's called **IMAGE SCRIMMAGE.**

And in case you didn't know,
a scrimmage is a duel, a battle.

Brian and I will take turns drawing creatures we think are the **greatest**, the **mightiest**, and the **most powerful** around. The most epic monster wins. There are only two rules: **start small** and **admit defeat** if you've been beaten.

Okay, let's begin!

A GNARLY STAG BEETLE

A STINGING SCORPION

7

You got me! **A cute kitty always wins.**
It can melt the heart of even the most awful beasts.

Hey, Alex!

Chapter 2:
CALL TO THE CLOUDS

Dear Blizz,

I'm lonely. I've got no one to talk to but frogs. If I can't find someone like me, I may have to leave Loch Ness.

Yours,
Vanessa

We have to help Nessie. She can't leave Loch Ness. That lake is her home. And it keeps her hidden.

Gang, it's time for a trip to Scotland.

CRYPTOTRON

DINNER ALONE

NO ONE LIKES MY TWEETS

#MELANCHOLY

I'll call Jack Saturday. Hopefully, he can give us a lift.

RING! RING!

Extra! Extra!

Can Jack bring home a win?

19

Well, hello. I'm Jack Saturday and I'm just about to win a very complicated game called the Rings of Alicornia. **Let me explain the rules.** But put your goggles on. Safety first!

Each team gets 10 rings: 9 silver and 1 gold. Players try to toss their silver rings on the opposing team's trees. To win, you must steal the other team's gold ring and land it on the Great Golden Spike, which I am just about to do.

Now, shhhh! I need to concentrate.

Chapter 3:
LONELY IN LOCH NESS

Ugh! Jack isn't picking up. How are we going to get to Scotland?

OOO
YES TUBE CUTE PIT BULL

Pump up your tires and slap on some bike shorts.

Wahoo!

If we can help her find **another creature like her,** maybe she'll be less lonely.

And we all know a happy cryptid is a hidden cryptid. We wouldn't want anyone to spot Nessie and discover her secrets, would we?

His name is Tobin Clover,
and he lives just across the water
in Ireland. His pot-of-gold can do this
neat little trick . . .

Chapter 4:
TOBIN'S MAGIC TRICK

Alex!

Hey, Tobin!

This is my boss, Blizz Richards, expert cryptozoologist. We have a tricky case that you may be able to help with.

Can we come inside?

FERGUS
THE CAT

HAT RACK

RESEARCH DEPARTMENT
SUPERCOMPUTER

Here's the situation.

Nessie wants to find others like her. Our plan is to travel 65 million years back in time.

DINO EGG

ALIEN EMBRYO

DICTIONARY IN ALL LANGUAGES

3-D GLASSES

PREHISTORIC BOAR SKULL

39

First, I have to think a happy thought.

For me, that means thinking about my cat, Fergus. He always makes me smile. He makes me sneeze, too, but right now I'm focusing on happier things.

And that makes a rainbow appear.

Next, I grab the strands of the rainbow and separate them, picking out two colors to combine.

41

By linking the strands in new combinations, I can travel to different places and times.

Like present-day New York or long-ago Easter Island.

I go back in time to right before a disaster is about to strike.

And I beam these objects to safety before they can be destroyed.

POOF!

It took a few tries for Tobin to get them where they wanted to go . . .

Chapter 5:
PREHISTORIC PROBLEMS

MESA

SWAMP
CYPRESS

TYRANNOSAURUS
REX

HORSETAILS

ANCIENT LOBSTER

ARMORED FISH

. . . and immediately got **separated!**

They landed in five different spots.

Chapter 6:
BLIZZ ON THE CASE

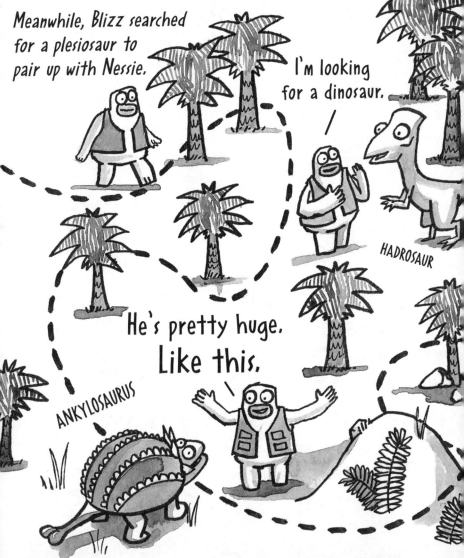

Meanwhile, Blizz searched for a plesiosaur to pair up with Nessie.

I'm looking for a dinosaur.

HADROSAUR

He's pretty huge. Like this.

ANKYLOSAURUS

Chapter 7:
A DANGEROUS LAND

But Nessie wasn't finding prehistoric waters nearly so friendly.

Who are these monsters?

Follow me!

DENSE JUNGLE

ICKY SWAMP

SCRUBLAND

HIGH MOUNTAINS

DRY DESERT

STEEP CLIFFS

Over here!

69

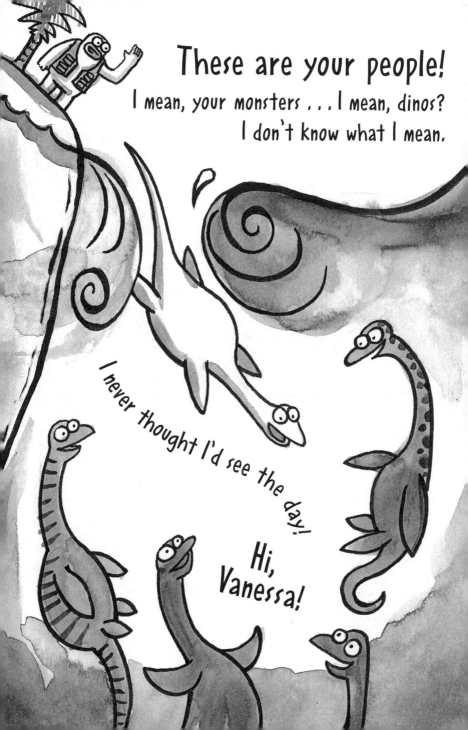

Meanwhile, Tobin had finally found someone who'd listen to him.

I was sightseeing in Pisa, Italy, when I saw some workers building a bell tower. It began to sink on one side. They wanted to fix it, but I told them it had character.

I like traveling back to ancient Alexandria, to read the scrolls in the library of knowledge. I once discovered a great old recipe for grape soda.

You know what the Sphinx looks like, right? Well, it actually used to have a nose! It fell off during an earthquake and I rescued it. I'm waiting for the right time to give it back.

And you've seen those sculptures on Easter Island? Well, I shouldn't say this, but they are actually hat racks for some other cryptids . . . the giants.

Protoceratops to the rescue!

Chapter 9:
DANGER IN THE DEEP

Nessie was finally making friends, too...

eaten!

out
th!

Oh yeah, it's like that all the time here.

Last week, our friend Jeff was that monster's lunch.

Nessie hightailed it out of the lake.

Hey, Blizz, we've got to get out of here.

It's too scary.

I want to go back home.

Now that I know what it's like for others like me, my life in the future doesn't seem so bad.

Plus, I'm not really alone after all.

I have friends so good they'll travel 65 million years back in time and risk their lives just to help me.

Great!
Now we just have to find Tobin and the rest of the team.

Chapter 10:
BACK TO THE FUTURE

Gunthar!
You saved us!

And you were paying attention to our image scrimmage lesson.

Tobin! Noodles! You found us? But how?

Let's just say this story could also be called *The Yeti Files 2: Loudest Cryptids of All Time.*

POOF!

Blizz, that was terribly dangerous, absolutely reckless, and totally **fun** and **rewarding!**

I better be going now.

But if you don't mind, **Noodles** is going to stay here with me. He's a great listener.

There is **another sea monster like you, Vanessa.**

And he lives with my cousin here in the present.

Here's a file
I put together
for you.

And met **Chester** the Chesapeake Bay monster, also known as Chessie.

Oh, my goodness!

Chapter 12:
NEW SURPRISES

· ·

Great job, team.
I'm going to surf the Internet.
There's some lasagna in the fridge
if you're hungry.

An urgent message
has interrupted the cryptotron.

We've been consulting our ancient manuscripts, and all signs point to one thing:

the return of the kraken!

THE KRAKEN

119

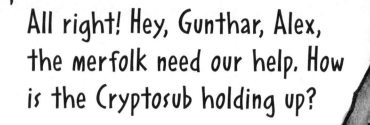

All right! Hey, Gunthar, Alex, the merfolk need our help. How is the Cryptosub holding up?

We gotta take care of that.
But first, let's call Jack!

Maybe his schedule has finally cleared up enough that he can help us get where we're needed. Our legs can't handle another bike ride, especially under water!